To Rylan, my hero. I love you deeply.

Thank you for your resiliency and fighting to stay with me.

I almost gave my life for you, but in the end you saved me.

So Teeny, So Tiny

for all the tiny but mighty warrior babies

Written by Lori McCorkle
Illustrated by Lily Liu

Once was a little boy, who came into the world as small as a **toy**. He was so teeny, so tiny but also so mighty.

He was born **strong**, he was born tough,
he was born a warrior, a **fighter**,
made with **love**, he was enough.

He grew and he grew with his **mom** by his side, **loving** him so deeply and praying every night.

Day after day his **doctors** would all say,
you can do hard things little man,

you are **part of Gods** plan.

So teeny,
so tiny and full of **grace**,
he fought the good fight,
and **won** at his own pace.

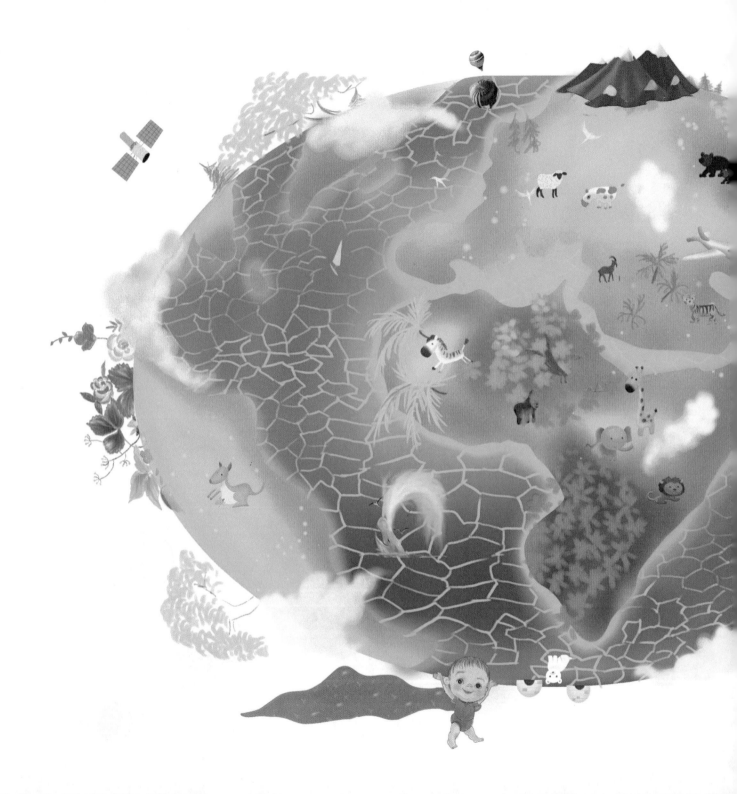

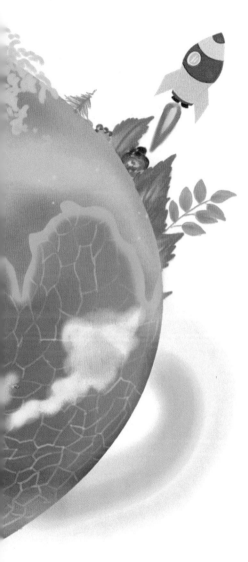

He is so **strong**,
he is so **tough**,
he can **conquer the world**,
he is made of Gods **good** stuff.

Brave, patient,
loving and smiley.

You are so **perfect**,
even so teeny so tiny.

So tiny,
so teeny,

and SO
very very **mighty!**

As a first time mom I was super nervous for my birth story as soon as I found out I was pregnant. I prayed continuously for my baby because I had such a rough start I felt like he needed extra prayers. 28 weeks and 3 days in, I had an emergency C Section because I was suffering from HELLP Syndrome. I checked into the hospital because I was in pain and less than 4 hours later I was laying on a table scared senseless of what was to come.

I simply wanted my son to survive and I knew it would be a battle. Rylan was 2 lbs and 5 oz, 16 inches long and born on 2/28/21. He was a tiny fighter from the start. Little did I know, he would teach me how to be patient, strong, an advocate for his life, and a warrior myself. All the grace is to God that my little miracle survived. Despite all the challenges that I don't want to focus on, despite all the time in hospitals and doctors offices, despite the pandemic that surged and despite being a single mom, Rylan showed me what it is to have faith, to completely lean on God when all hope is lost.

It is the worst imaginable pain to watch your child and feel helpless. It is the strongest joy to watch them overcome the odds and become a miracle you only hear about. I wrote this book to celebrate him, to celebrate all other children who fight any battle from early on, to celebrate the mommas, the families, doctors and the friends effected.

So Teeny, So Tiny is a celebration of overcoming lifes most difficult journey at a young age. God Bless each of you who have walked this path and those who may walk it in the future. You are a warrior.

Lori McCorkle is mom to Rylan (1) and dog mom to Moose. She resides in Madison, AL where she works as a Purchasing Program Manager for a Defense Contractor. She is a part time editor and finally decided to publish her first Children's book after the birth of her son in hope to inspire him one day to live out his dreams.

Lori McCorkle

Lily(Li) Liu is not only a highly educated and trained artist, she also teaches art and resides in France. She has been working with authors all over the world for over a decade. She is also the illustrator of best selling books on Amazon including *Her Body Can* and *Where Is My House*, which have won the top Overall in Children's books on Amazon.

Lily Liu

THANK YOU

The fact that entering this world is a fight for some children is heartbreaking. Thankfully, God blessed Rylan with a fighting spirit and surrounded him with the best doctors, nurses, and staff. I would like to thank the nurses, doctors, therapist, security, and staff at UAB Children's Hospital CVICU unit and HSV Hospitals Women and Children's division in Alabama.

Special thank you to my mom and dad better known as Grammy and Papa for helping me raise Rylan this past year. Not only did you give him the opportunity to live his first year with extra unconditional love and mentorship but you gave me relief, naps, and support!

To my brother and sister and their families for helping me when they could and offering unwavering support even during my lowest of lows. Angela, in the midst of one of my worst days you told me I don't have to be perfect. You said to keep Rylan safe and just love him like I do and we will make it. It changed my course of thinking and took a huge burden off my shoulders. Nathan, when I was in dire need of help to get my son to the right place, you put me in contact with the person who got us to where we needed to be. I truly believe that helped Rylan get home weeks sooner. I had answers within days and a plan to get him well and home.

To the nurse who guided me through my surgery and delivery. I do not know your name, but you will forever live in my heart for comforting me and making the situation as calm as possible.

To my dear friends who supported me mentally, emotionally, spiritually and physically during the hardest time in my life...thank you for sticking by me.

To Lily for bringing this small dream of mine to life with your gorgeous illustrations.

To family friends for sending cards filled with support and well wishes and gifts. These gestures really helped me feel like I wasn't alone.

Dr. John Wheeler
Savannah Helms
Ady Meschke
Brittany Huey

Made in the USA
Las Vegas, NV
08 December 2023

82324703R00017